MY HOUSEPLANTS WHISPER WISDOM

Written & Illustrated by: **TASSIA SCHREINER**
Artwork in collaboration with: Anhelina Stepanova

THEY WHISPER WORDS
OF WISDOM
AND I KNOW WHERE
THEY'LL ALWAYS BE.

You have to bloom
You have to bloom
You have to bloom
You have to bloom
You have to bloom

ALOE HA

Made in the USA
Monee, IL
15 March 2022

92928311R00019